Gargoylz

on the Go!

Burchett & Vogler

illustrated by Leighton Noyes

RED FOX

GARGOYLZ ON THE GO!

A RED FOX BOOK 978 1 849 41184 4

First published in Great Britain by Red Fox,
an imprint of Random House Children's Books
A Random House Group Company

This edition published 2010

1 3 5 7 9 10 8 6 4 2

Series created and developed by Amber Caravéo

The Random House Group Limited supports the Forest Stewardship Council
(FSC), the leading international forest certification organization. All our titles
that are printed on Greenpeace-approved FSC-certified paper carry the FSC
logo. Our paper procurement policy can be found at
www.rbooks.co.uk/environment

Mixed Sources
Product group from well-managed
forests and other controlled sources
www.fsc.org Cert no. TT-COC-2139
© 1996 Forest Stewardship Council

Set in Bembo Schoolbook

Red Fox Books are published by Random House Children's Books,
61–63 Uxbridge Road, London W5 5SA

www.**kids**at**randomhouse**.co.uk
www.**rbooks**.co.uk

Addresses for companies within The Random House Group Limited can be
found at: www.randomhouse.co.uk/offices.htm

THE RANDOM HOUSE GROUP Limited Reg. No. 954009

A CIP catalogue record for this book is available from the British Library.

Printed and bound in Great Britain by CPI Bookmarque, Croydon, CR0 4TD

Gargoylz

on the Go!

Gargoylz: grotesque stone
   creatures found on old
buildings, spouting rainwater
   from the guttering.
Sometimes seen causing
   mischief and mayhem
before scampering away
   over rooftops.

Read all the Gargoylz adventures!

For Christopher May - who would have designed a much better go-kart for Ben.
- **Burchett & Vogler**

For James and Fran, with love x
- **Leighton Noyes**

Hello, I'm the Web Gargoyle.
Look out for me – I'll be hiding in one of the pictures in the book.
When you spot me, be sure to make a note of the secret codeword I'm holding.
The codeword unlocks a secret level of the amazing Gargoylz game on our fabulous website at
www.gargolyz.co.uk

Oldacre Primary School

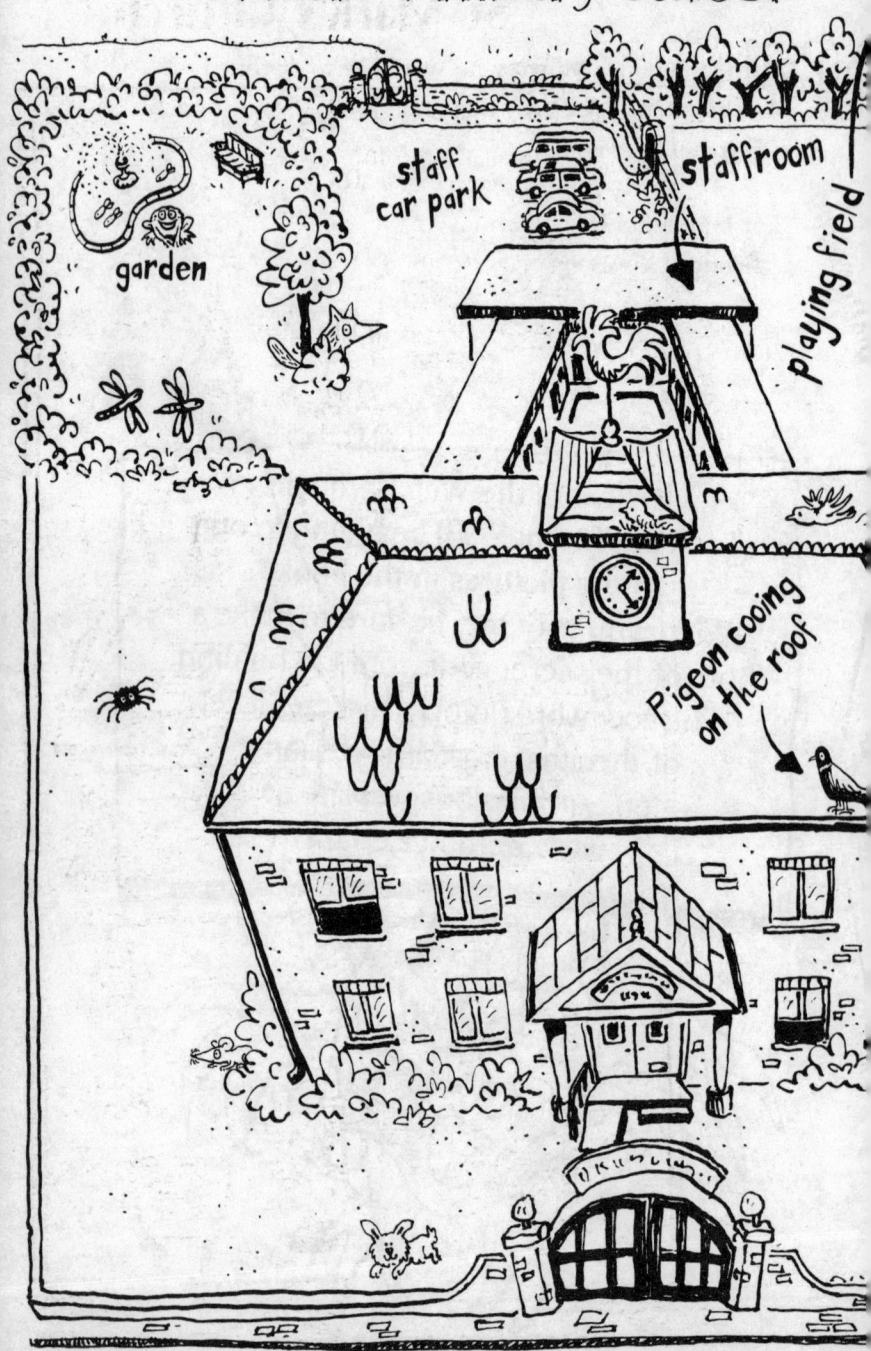

St Mark's Church

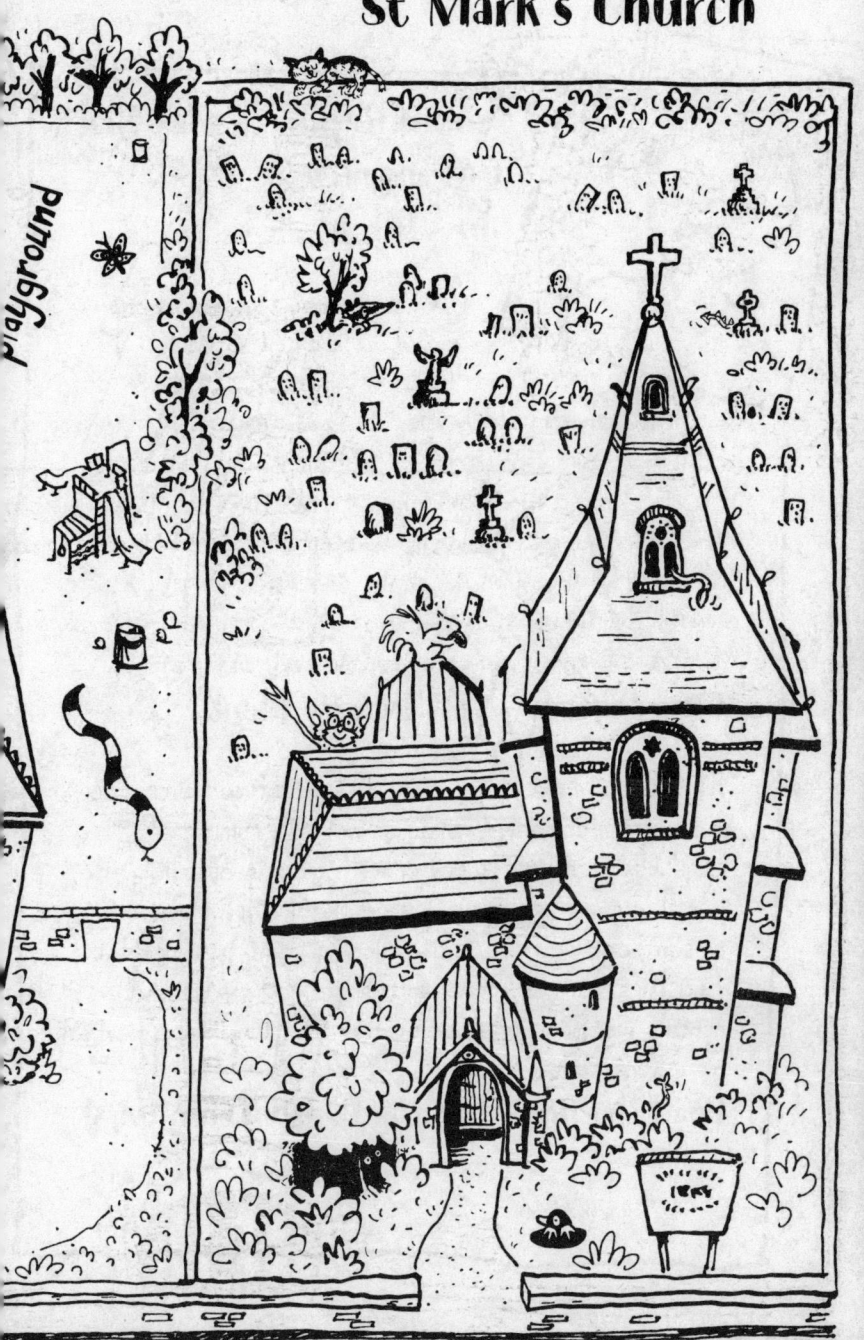

Playground

School Report - Max Black
Days absent: 0
Days late: 0

Max is never afraid to make a contribution to history lessons. His demonstration of a battering ram using a broom and a bucket was very realistic, although the resulting hole in the classroom door was not ideal.

I worry that Max only seems to play with Ben Neal, but he assures me he has a lot of friends at the local church.

Class teacher - Miss Deirdre Bleet

Max Black's behaviour this term has been outrageous. He has repeatedly broken school rule number 739: boys must not tell 'knock knock' jokes in assembly. He is still playing pranks with Ben Neal. Mrs Pumpkin is absent again after the exploding paint pot incident. And Mrs Simmer, the head dinner lady, says the mincing machine has never been the same since he fed his maths test into it.

Head teacher - Hagatha Hogsbottom (Mrs)

School Report - Ben Neal

Days absent: 0

Days late: 0

This term Ben has
been very inventive in PE.
However, attempting to tightrope-walk
across the hall was a little dangerous
– and used up all the skipping ropes.
He spends far too much time in class
looking out of the window and waving at
the gravestones in the churchyard. He
would be better learning his spellings – a
word he insists on writing as 'spellingz'.

Class teacher - Miss Deirdre Bleet

Ben Neal is always polite, but I am deeply concerned
about his rucksack. It often looks very full – and
not with school books, I am certain. It has sometimes
been seen to wriggle and squirm. I suspect that he
is keeping a pet in there. If so, it is outrageous and
there will be trouble.

Head teacher - Hagatha Hogsbottom (Mrs)

Contents

1. Holiday Plans

Max Black screeched up to his best friend's house on his imaginary spy turbo-rocket – codename: bicycle.

Awesome, he thought. *It's half-term. There's no school for a week and I'm going to spend the whole day with Ben.*

Ben Neal flung open the door. He had a huge grin on his face. "Ready to make holiday plans with the gargoylz, Agent Black?" he said.

"Ready, Agent Neal!" replied Max eagerly. "Get your bike and we'll go and see them."

1

The gargoylz were Max and Ben's top-secret friends. Everyone else in Oldacre thought they were just ugly stone statues carved all over the church next to the boys' school. Only Max and Ben knew that the mischievous little creatures were alive – and ready to play all sorts of tricks, using their special powers.

A dreadful screeching noise suddenly filled the house. "Has someone trodden on a cat?" Max asked.

"It's worse than that," said Ben, covering his ears. "Arabella's singing!"

"That's given me a cool idea," said Max, his eyes wide with mischief. "Before we see the gargoylz, let's practise our secret agent skills by spying on your sister."

Ben gave him a high-five. "Brilliant plan!" he exclaimed.

Grabbing their superspy info-collecting kit — codename: notebooks and pencils — they crept along the hall towards the ghastly sound.

"It's coming from the dining room," hissed Max. "She mustn't see us."

They peered through the crack in the door. Max activated his spy radar: pigtails bobbing, simpering smile, screeching voice. He knew what that meant. It was

Ben's sister, Enemy Agent Arabella Neal, codename: Manic Monitor.

"Enemy agent has window open," he whispered.

"Window open," repeated Ben, scribbling down the information. "She must have an evil plan to deafen everyone in Oldacre."

"I heard that!" snapped Arabella. She yanked open the door, and Max and Ben tumbled into the room. Arabella stomped off into the lounge.

"Plan failed, Agent Black," said Ben, picking himself up.

"We must try again," said Max, "this time in super silent mode."

Quick as cheetahs the boys scampered after her and ducked down behind the sofa.

Arabella was reading a magazine.

"Enemy agent scanning secret papers," reported Max.

"Scanning secret papers," repeated Ben as he scrawled down the words.

"Go away!" Arabella said grumpily.

She turned on the TV and started watching a programme about make-up. "That should get rid of them!" she muttered to herself.

Like shadows, the boys dived under the coffee table to get nearer.

"Plan working," hissed Ben. "She has no idea we're here."

"Enemy agent studying cosmetics," said Max. "She must be planning a dastardly disguise."

"Dastardly disguise!" repeated Ben, making notes. "She certainly needs it to cover that ugly face."

"MUM!" shrieked Arabella. Mrs Neal appeared at the door. "Max and Ben are tormenting me."

"We were only spying on her," Ben called from under the coffee table.

"Leave her alone," said his mother.

"I've got a job for you two."

"That doesn't sound like fun,"
whispered Max. "We're meant to be on
half-term holiday."

Mrs Neal shooed them into the kitchen.

"You can make some fairy cakes for me
while I do the housework."

The boys looked at her in disgust.

"Oozy mud cakes then," she said
quickly. "Aprons on!"

"Mum!" gasped Ben in horror.

"All the top chefs wear aprons," said Mrs Neal, handing the boys two bright pinnies.

"Not covered in flowers, they don't,"

muttered Max. He stopped when he saw Ben's mum produce a bowl of chocolate squares and put it over a pan on the cooker to melt. Then she picked up a duster and went off into the hall.

The boys sniffed the delicious smell of melting chocolate.

"What are we waiting for?" yelled Ben.

They read the recipe and began to measure out the ingredients. Max tossed the sugar into the mixing bowl – and all over the kitchen.

"Flour sifted!" said Ben, holding out a bowl. "What's next?"

"Butter bomb!" Max announced. He dropped the butter into the bowl, sending a cloud of white flour into the air.

"Eggs surprise!" yelled Ben, splattering the eggs into the mixture and then fishing out the shells.

Max grabbed the whisk and began to mix everything up into a gooey gloop.

Mrs Neal came in again. "Did you have to make so much mess?" she complained. She poured the melted chocolate into the mixture. "Now stir this in – carefully – while I find some paper cake cases." She went to rummage around in a cupboard.

Ben plunged his finger into the bowl and scooped a big blob of chocolatey goo into his mouth. "Just testing," he said.

"Me too," said Max, sticking a spoon in.

"Fantastic!" Ben took another helping.

"Yumtastic!" agreed Max, licking his lips and diving in again.

At last Mrs Neal appeared with the cake cases. She gawped into the bowl. "There's not enough left for even one cake!"

"We'd better finish it off then," said Ben helpfully.

"We wouldn't want it to go to waste," added Max.

Before Ben's mum could protest, the boys had scraped the bowl clean.

"We're off to play now," announced Ben.

"No you're not," said his mother crossly. "You're going to wash everything up. And I'll be back in a minute to check."

When she'd gone, Ben looked at the bowl. "This looks clean enough to put away," he said.

"You're right," agreed Max, licking the whisk in his hand. "None of it needs washing."

11

He began throwing spoons into the drawer.

"I can't hear water running!" they heard Mrs Neal shout from the hall.

"Better get on with it," groaned Ben.

Max ran warm water into the sink and added half a bottle of washing-up liquid. He looked at the mountain of bubbles spilling out. "This is the biggest ocean on Jupiter, and here comes an asteroid." He dropped the sieve into the foam.

"And some shooting stars," yelled Ben, pelting the bubbles with the spoons and whisk. Water splashed all over the counter – and the boys.

"Watch out for the crashing spaceship!" shouted Max, standing on a chair and dropping the bowl in. A huge wave washed out and soaked the floor.

"Boys!" Mrs Neal stood at the door, a look of horror on her face. "What have you done to my kitchen?"

"We're playing Alien Rocket Disaster," explained Ben patiently.

"I've had enough of your tricks," snapped his mother. "I'm phoning Mrs Black. You can go to Max's house for a while."

She grabbed the telephone off the wall. After a short conversation, she shepherded the boys to the door. "She's expecting you. Take your bikes and go straight there. We've decided that if you're not there in fifteen minutes you'll be grounded. You won't see each other for the rest of the week!"

Max and Ben looked at each other in horror, grabbed their bikes and rucksacks and shot off down the road.

"Secret plan alert, Agent Neal!" called Max. "Let's make a detour past the church and pick up the gargoylz. There should be time."

They arrived at St Mark's church, shot up the path and stopped by the porch with a squeal of brakes.

Max peered over at their school. "This is the best way to see Oldacre Primary," he said. "With the gates firmly locked and us on the outside!"

"Greetingz!" came a growly purr. "I've been looking out for you."

A monkey-faced gargoyle was peeping over the church porch at them.

"Hi, Toby!" called Max in delight.

"We would have been here sooner,"

explained Ben, "but there was a tidal wave in my kitchen."

"And we can't stop for long," said Max. "We'll be in big trouble if we don't get to my house soon."

Toby's face fell.

"But you can come with us," said Max, "and anyone else who's around."

Toby beamed. "Spluttering gutterz!" he said, using his secret power to fly down and join them. "I'd love to come."

A small snort of fire rose up from behind a headstone and a dragony gargoyle scrambled out. "And me!" he said. "As long as there are no tidal waves in your kitchen, Max. They might put my flames out."

"I don't think we'll be allowed near the sink, Azzan," said Ben. "Anyone else coming?"

"Me, please." Barney was right behind Azzan. The spines down his stony back quivered with excitement.

"Jump into our rucksacks then," Max told them. "We've got to be quick. My mum's expecting us in three minutes and we'll be grounded if we're late."

Pop! A grinning gargoyle appeared out of thin air, shaking his shaggy mane

happily. Zack's ability to become invisible was very useful when it came to playing tricks.

"Me too!" he yelled. "See you there!" **Pop!** He disappeared again.

The boys arrived at Max's house with seconds to spare. Mrs Black was waiting for them at the front door.

"You've just made it," she said sternly, checking her watch. "Now go and play quietly upstairs."

Max's rucksack wriggled. "We will!" came Toby's loud, growly voice.

"We're always quiet," added Azzan.

"Who said that?" asked Mrs Black, looking around.

"Well, it wasn't me or Ben," answered Max. "You must be hearing things, Mum!"

With that they bolted up the stairs.

"I can't think of any quiet games,"
said Ben when they were safely in Max's
bedroom.

"We could watch TV," said Toby.

"Or read comics," suggested Barney.

"I know a really quiet game," declared
Zack, jumping up excitedly. "Chase!
Catch me."

Pop! He disappeared, and the next
moment the bedroom door opened and
shut with a crash.

"Great!" said Azzan, bounding to the
door. "I love Chase."

Toby and Barney rushed after him.

Max blocked their way. "No," he cried. "Chase is far too noisy."

"And you might be seen by humans," added Ben. "We've got to stop Zack before he gets us into trouble."

"Whatever he does, Mum'll think it's us," said Max. "We'll be grounded for a year!"

The boys dashed out onto the landing and listened hard. Scampering footsteps could be heard going down the stairs.

"Quick!" yelled Max. "He's getting away."

They raced after Zack, pounding downstairs into the hall and running straight into Mrs Black, who was carrying a basket of washing. Vests and socks flew up into the air.

"You boys are horrendous!" exclaimed
Mrs Black, struggling out from under the
pile of clothes. She had a pair of pants
stuck on her head. Max and Ben burst out
laughing. Growly gargoyle chuckles rose
up from under the shoe rack, where the
boys could see the tips of three stony tails.
The gargoylz had come down to see the
fun. Then a dreadful pong filled the air.

"Uh-oh," whispered Ben. "Barney's got
so excited he's let off a bottom burp!"

Barney's secret power was great, but
sometimes his dreadful smells came out
accidentally.

"This washing doesn't smell very clean," said Max quickly before his mum blamed them.

With a face like thunder, Mrs Black reached for the phone. "I'm calling Ben's mum to come and take him home," she said, pants slipping over her ears. "You two go out into the garden and stay there until she comes."

Max and Ben ran down to the trees at the bottom of the garden. They heard a swishing in the grass and saw that the gargoylz had joined them. They all rolled about laughing.

"Your mum looked so funny, Max!" chortled Azzan.

"Panty hat! Panty hat!" chanted Zack.

"I haven't laughed so much since we

ate the icing off the vicar's birthday cake and covered it in toothpaste instead," wheezed Toby, slapping his sides.

When the chuckles had died down at last, Zack held up a packet of biscuits. "Look what I found in the kitchen!" he said, sharing them out.

"Custard creamz!" sighed Barney. "My favourites."

Azzan blew a small flame in the air and held his biscuit up to it. "Breathing fire is a useful secret power," he announced, "Good for melting the custard."

"They were scrumptious!" exclaimed Zack when the packet was empty.

"Secret mission, Agent Neal," said Max. "Sneak into enemy headquarters – the kitchen – and get more supplies."

"I'm with you, Agent Black!" declared Ben.

"We're coming too," Azzan told them.

"Last one there is a Jammy Dodger!" shouted Ben, and he set off towards the house, Max and the gargoylz close behind.

They slowed down to superspy crawling speed as they got near the open back door.

"Make sure the coast is clear," hissed Max.

They crept forward and stopped dead when they heard voices in the kitchen.

"They're driving me mad!"

"Me too."

"That's our mums," whispered Max.

"Are they talking about us?" asked Ben.

"Can't be!" Max inched forward towards the back step. "They probably mean Jessica and Arabella. My little sister is the most annoying thing in the history of most annoying things!"

They heard Max's mum sigh. "They're only out of mischief when they're eating," she said. "And not always then."

"There's not enough food in the world to keep them from causing trouble," put in Mrs Neal.

"There's only one thing for it," said Mrs Black firmly. "We have to find those boys a hobby."

Max and Ben looked

at each other in amazement. "They are talking about us!" gasped Max.

"They think we cause trouble!" said Ben in disbelief.

"Yoga's very calming," Mrs Black went on. "We might get a bit of peace and quiet if they do that."

"What's yoga?" demanded Toby. "Can you eat it?"

"It's something mums do," said Ben. "They stretch their legs and tie themselves in knots." He pulled a face.

"We've got to think of our own hobby," said Max, "and fast – before our mothers make us do yoga."

"Fire-breathing!" suggested Azzan. "Then we can practise together."

"That would be great," said Max,

"if we were dragons."

"You could learn to fly," put in Toby. "Then you'll be just like me."

"That would be great too," said Ben, "if we had wings."

"Disappearing!" Zack declared, popping in and out of sight.

"Well . . ." said Ben.

Max jumped up. "I've just remembered something awesome, Agent Neal. They've got kayaking classes on Oldacre Lake."

"Double awesome, Agent Black!" Ben punched the air. "And our mums might just agree! Come on . . ."

They bounded into the kitchen, making their mothers jump.

"We were just talking about finding you both a hobby," said Mrs Black. "There's a nice quiet embroidery class—"

"We'd like to go kayaking on Oldacre Lake!" burst in Max.

"I'm not sure about that," said Mrs Black. "Embroidery would be more likely to calm you down."

The boys were horrified.

"That's so girly, Mum!" gasped Max.

"We'd be sick all over our stitches," warned Ben.

Suddenly Max had a brilliant idea.

"I've changed my mind," he said. "It sounds lovely,"

"What!" Ben gaped at him in horror.

"Just think of it, Ben," Max went on, giving his friend a secret wink. "After sitting peacefully with our needles and thread, we'll be full of energy to play lots of pranks!"

Their mothers looked at each other in alarm.

"I suppose kayaking would tire them out," said Mrs Neal quickly.

"And it will keep them busy for a few hours," agreed Mrs Black. "We'll arrange it, boys."

Max and Ben jumped into their imaginary superspy canoes and rowed outside at turbo speed.

"We're going kayaking!" Ben told their waiting friends. "Come and watch."

The gargoylz jumped in the air with delight.

"This is going to be the most brilliant half-term ever!" exclaimed Max.

2. All Aboard!

The next morning Max and Ben zoomed along to Oldacre Lake in their imaginary spy hover-cars. A crowd of children were eagerly waiting by a row of kayaks that lay upside down on the grass.

"Any sign of the gargoylz?" asked Ben, looking around.

"Not yet," said Max.

He scanned the area. Suddenly his spy radar whirred into action: clean swimsuits, pink ribbons, shrill voices. He knew what that meant. It was two enemy agents – Lucinda Tellingly and Poppy Parker.

They were
standing as
close to the
instructor
as they
could, eagerly
listening to every
word he said.

Max groaned
and pointed at the girls. "I've spotted
something really nasty."

"They'll be useless at kayaking," said
Ben cheerfully. "We'll be able to paddle
away from them, no problem."

"Good point," said Max with a grin.
"We'll probably just hear terrified shrieks
behind us when they sink."

The instructor gathered everybody
round. "My name's Gary," he said. "Now
everyone's here we'll make a start. First
you all need to put on these wetsuits."

He handed out some black rubbery

suits. Everyone stripped down to their swimming costumes and squeezed into them.

Lucinda pointed at Max. "Max and Ben look like a pair of stupid sea lions in the zoo."

"I wish we had some fish to throw to them," laughed Poppy.

"Don't worry, girls," said Max. "You'll soon find some when you fall out of your kayaks."

Before Lucinda could protest, Gary put up his hand for silence. "Take a life jacket and a paddle each. But no rushing for the kayaks!" He looked sternly at Max and Ben, who had pulled on their life jackets, snatched their oars and dived for the nearest boats. "Before we get in the water I have to tell you a few simple rules ..."

"Boring!" whispered Ben. "Too much like school."

"Let's have a paddle battle while we're waiting," suggested Max. He whirled his paddle around his head while Ben leaped about, swishing the air.

". . . and nobody messes around with the paddles." Gary glared at them. "I can see I'll have to keep an eye on you two."

Lucinda and Poppy tutted and shook their heads.

"We'll show those girls," hissed Max, "as soon as we're on the lake."

"Has anybody been kayaking before?" asked Gary.

To Max and Ben's horror, Lucinda's hand shot up. "I have, sir. Every year on holiday since I was three."

"I wish we'd never thought of kayaking," muttered Max.

"It's going to be awful with Lucinda showing off," agreed Ben.

Just then, Max heard a growly voice calling his name from the bushes behind them. He glanced over his shoulder and a big grin spread over his face. "It's going to be fun after all," he whispered, nudging Ben in the ribs.

A cheeky monkey face was peeping out through the leaves. "Toby!" gasped Ben. "Good to see you." The little gargoyle scuttled over to the line of upturned kayaks and disappeared underneath the nearest one.

"Now, I want you to take a kayak each," said their instructor, "put it in the water and climb aboard."

"I'll demonstrate how it's done," said Lucinda loudly as everyone made a beeline for the boats. "You can all watch if you like."

To the boys' horror she made straight for the kayak where Toby was hiding.

"Emergency action stations, Agent Neal," cried Ben, sticking his paddle out in front of Lucinda. "Toby mustn't be discovered!"

Lucinda tried to dodge Ben's flailing paddle, lost her balance and fell into a patch of reeds. Max quickly grabbed Toby's kayak.

"So sorry, Lucinda," said Ben, trying not to laugh as Poppy helped her up. "I was just practising for when we're on the water."

Lucinda scowled and stomped off with Poppy. Soon she was getting into her kayak and shouting loud instructions to everyone else.

Max and Ben carried their boats to the edge of the lake and slid them into the water. After a lot of wobbling and splashing they managed to slide their legs into their kayaks.

"Greetingz!" Toby's head popped up next to Max. "I didn't realize boats could be so much fun. I can rock this one like a fairground ride!"

He scampered about, making the kayak wobble alarmingly.

"Stop it, Toby!" hissed Max, clinging to the sides. "We don't want Gary coming over."

Suddenly Ben gave a shout. "There's something attacking my feet. Help!"

Max paddled over to him.

"Sit still, you scurvy sea sausage," came a squawk from Ben's boat. "You'll sink my ship."

A stony head with a big hooked beak poked out of the kayak.

"Ira!" exclaimed Ben in delight. "I didn't know you were here too."

"I wouldn't miss a trip on the high seas!" declared Ira. "You'll need a clever pirate like me on this voyage. There could be terrible storms – or ferocious creatures in the deep."

Ira looked more like an eagle than a parrot and had never been on the ocean

in his life, but he was convinced that he
was a fierce pirate sea captain.

"I'm sure we'll be all right," called Max.
"After all, this is only a little lake . . ."

"But you never know what's lurking in
the deep," said Ira solemnly as he hopped
onto the prow of the boat and peered into
the water. "Or the shallows," he added.

There was a loud quack from the
bank. Ira jumped in fright and nearly
fell overboard. "All hands on deck!" he
squawked, flapping his wings in panic.
"Monster ahoy!"

"It's not a monster," Ben
assured him. "It's just a
harmless duck."

Ira glared at the
duck, which slid
into the water
and swam away
hurriedly. Then,
lifting a wing

to his eyes, he
scanned the water
and spotted Gary
coming alongside.
"Enemy on the
port bow!" he shrieked,
and disappeared inside the kayak with a
loud screech.

"What was making those silly
squawking noises?" said Gary sternly. "It
sounded as if it was coming from one of
your kayaks."

Max and Ben froze. Was Gary going to
discover Ira?

Ben came to the rescue. He gave
Gary his wide-eyed innocent look. It
always fooled the dinner ladies at school,
who gave him extra strawberry tart. "A
strange-looking pigeon just flew over," he
said helpfully. "It must have been that."

"Strange-looking pigeon indeed!" came
a muffled voice from the bottom of the

boat. "I'll make you walk the plank for that!"

"There it goes again," said Max. "I think it can talk."

Gary peered up into the sky, scratched his head and paddled off. "Gather round, everybody!" he called. "The first thing you're going to learn is how to right yourselves if your kayaks capsize."

Everyone rowed up, eager to start

their lesson.

"Lucinda – you go first," said Gary.

Giving a smug smile, Lucinda flicked her paddle in front of her, rolled sideways and disappeared under the surface, upturning the kayak. The next instant she'd popped up on the other side. Everyone clapped.

"Now find some space and you can all have a go," said Gary.

"Anyone can do that," said Ben. He brought his paddle down into the water with a great splash, rolled sideways and disappeared. The kayak lay upside down, but there was no sign of Ben.

Max rowed over and tapped the bottom of the kayak with his paddle. "Calling Agent Neal!" he shouted. "Are you all right?"

SECRET CODEWORD: DOG

Ben's head popped up out of the water next to the kayak. "I'm fine," he spluttered, wriggling desperately to pull himself upright. "Most of me is wedged inside the boat." He gave a great heave and the kayak turned the right way up.

A very cross-looking Ira struggled up from inside the kayak, an eel wrapped round his beak. He shook it off into the water. "You should have warned your captain that we were going down," he said, waggling a wing severely at Ben.

"Sorry," said Ben with a grin. "But you should have been listening to the instructor. Your turn to roll, Agent Black."

Max shook his head. "No time," he said. "It looks like we're off."

Gary was leading the way across the lake. "Follow me. We're going to do a circuit."

The class followed.

"Let's stay at the back, Agent Neal," suggested Max. "That way the gargoylz won't have to keep out of sight."

"Good thinking, Agent Black," replied Ben. "We can all have some fun."

Toby and Ira scrambled out onto the prow of their boats and sat there looking like ugly grinning figureheads.

"Race you to that island in the middle!" declared Toby. "Our kayak is the *Flying Monkey* and we're going to win."

"Not with me at the helm of Max's fine craft," declared Ira. "I name this ship

the *Jolly Parrot* – and it'll
be the fastest on the seven seas."

"Agreed," said Max. "But no
wriggling."

Max and Ben paddled as fast as they
could, trying to be first to the island.
"More speed!" commanded Ira as the two
boats ploughed through the water in the
opposite direction to the rest of the class.
"Hoist the mainsail! Row for your life."

He turned a beady eye on Ben. "Put
your back into it, you lazy sea dog." Then
he jumped up and down on the kayak,
making it wobble.

"Stop it!" yelled Ben.

"Faster!" screeched Ira.

"There's only one way to shut you up," muttered Ben. He stuck his paddle in the water and rolled the kayak over.

When Ben and Ira reappeared, they were both dripping wet and covered in lake slime.

"Who did that?" demanded Ira, shaking his stony feathers crossly. "If I catch the scurvy knave who tried to scupper me ship, I'll put him in a barrel and throw him in the ocean."

"It was me," Ben admitted, picking a bit of water lily out of his ear. "I know I deserve to be punished, Captain, but if you stick me in a barrel there'll be no one to paddle the kayak – er . . . your magnificent ship."

"And we lost the race," said Ira. "Their galleon has reached the finishing post."

The *Flying Monkey* was bobbing about near the island, and Max and Toby were shaking with laughter at the sight of the two dripping sailors.

"I reckon it's their turn for a soaking," muttered Ben.

"Well said, shipmate!" shrieked Ira, flapping his wings gleefully. "Full speed ahead. Attack the enemy vessel."

"Let the battle of Oldacre Lake begin!" yelled Ben, paddling furiously towards his friends.

Before Max and Toby could get out of the way, Ben lifted the paddle and brought it down hard on the lake, sending up a huge shower of water all over them.

"Dangling drainpipes!" laughed Toby. "We're not standing for this."

Max scooped up a paddleful of weed and flicked it at Ben. Toby hung over the side, sucked up a great mouthful of water and spat it over Ira. Soon the two kayaks had disappeared in a cloud of spray and flying pondweed.

"Look at Max and Ben!" came a piercing voice. "I'm telling."

The boys stopped mid-battle. Lucinda and Poppy were paddling towards them, followed by Gary the instructor.

"Uh-oh," groaned Max. "We're in big trouble now."

"Hide, gargoylz!" hissed Ben.

Toby dived down into Max's boat but Ira ran up and down Ben's kayak, squawking in panic.

"Man the lifeboats!" he shrieked. "We're going to be boarded."

"You mustn't be seen," Max called urgently. "Pretend to be a duck."

Ira immediately dived for the island and disappeared among the reeds.

Gary came alongside the boys' kayaks and brought his boat to a halt.

"I've already told you – no messing about," he said sternly.

"No messing about," repeated Lucinda and

Poppy, wagging their fingers.

"Quark! Quark!" came a parroty squawk from the reeds.

Gary whipped round in surprise and began to push the reeds aside with his paddle. "I've never heard a call like that before," he said.

Max and Ben looked at each other in horror. Was he going to find Ira?

"That's the funny-looking pigeon I told you about," said Ben quickly. "But you mustn't disturb it. They can be dangerous – very snappy beaks."

"Repel enemy boats!" squawked Ira. "I mean . . . **Quark, quark!**"

"They're very rare, you know," added Max as Gary backed off in astonishment. "We're lucky to hear one at this time of year."

"I hope this isn't some trick," said their

instructor doubtfully. "You two had better pull your socks up. Try to behave more like Lucinda and Poppy here." He paddled off to join the rest of the class.

Lucinda and Poppy grinned triumphantly at the boys.

"We don't play games . . ." said Lucinda, tossing her ponytail.

"Or get ourselves in trouble," added Poppy smugly.

Max groaned. "We're going to be stuck with these awful girls for ever," he whispered to Ben.

"**Quark, quark!**" came Ira's voice. "Launch an attack."

There was a fluttering of stony wings from the reeds and a small dark cloud appeared in the sunny sky. It floated directly over the girls' heads and – **whoosh!** – rain pelted down on them.

"Ira's using his secret power," said Ben in delight.

Lucinda and Poppy let out horrified shrieks and paddled away as quickly as they could. But the little cloud followed, throwing water down on the girls until their hair was plastered to their heads. Blinded by the rain, they crashed into each other and capsized.

"Enemy defeated!" squawked Ira from the reeds as the cloud floated off and disappeared.

The girls bobbed to the surface. Gary paddled over, his face stern.

"I thought you two would behave," he

said to them. "But you're as bad as the boys."

Lucinda and Poppy sheepishly followed him towards the rest of the class.

Max and Ben burst out laughing.

"You can come out now, Ira!" Ben called into the reeds.

"That was a great idea, making it rain on Lucinda and Poppy," said Max as the parroty gargoyle jumped back onto Ben's kayak.

"Serves the simpering seadogz right!" he squawked.

"Dangling drainpipes," shouted Toby, popping his head up from Max's boat. "I haven't laughed so much since Zack mooed down the vicar's chimney and he thought there was a cow in the fireplace."

"And now there's only one thing to do," yelled Max, digging his paddle into the water. "Have more kayaking fun."

"Awesome!" cried the gargoylz as Ben set off after him.

3. Superspy Dog Walkers

The next morning Ben woke up and
jumped out of bed. He was hungry for
his breakfast and feeling full of beans.
He dashed downstairs, still in his Batman
pyjamas, and burst into the kitchen.

Mum and Arabella were sitting at the
table. There was a heap of steaming toast
in front of them. In one skilful movement,
Ben slid across the floor and landed on
a chair. He splattered butter and jam on
some toast and crammed it into
his mouth.

"That's better," he mumbled.

"I was about to die from hunger."

Arabella sniffed disapprovingly. "Some of us bothered to get dressed before we came down," she said.

"Too busy," said Ben. "What have you got planned for me today, Mum? More kayaking?" He grabbed two pieces of bread and the packet of Golden Flakes and made himself a jammy crunchy sandwich.

"I'm not made of money!" exclaimed Mrs Neal. "You can do it again later this week. Anyway I've got something really fun for you and Max to do today – and you'll also be doing a good deed for someone, so everyone wins."

"Anything that keeps him out of my way will be a good deed," sniffed Arabella.

"What is it?" demanded Ben, ignoring his sister.

"Mrs MacDonald from my painting class phoned me this morning," his mother told him. "She has a bad cold and needs someone to walk her dogs." She got up and began to clear the table. "I said that you and Max would take them round the park."

"Cool," cried Ben. "I've always wanted to be a dog walker."

"I've spoken to Mrs Black, and Max will be round any minute," said Mrs Neal. "So you'd better get dressed."

Ben flew up the stairs.

"And don't forget to wash first," yelled his mum after him. "And brush your teeth."

Ben was just pulling on his trainers when the doorbell rang. He slid down the banister, landed on the mat and flung open the front door.

Max stood there, a huge grin on his face. "Ready for Superspy Mission: Dog Walking, Agent Neal?" he asked.

"Ready, Agent Black," said Ben. "We just need to collect the Superspy Mission sniffing equipment, codename: dogs."

They sped off to Mrs MacDonald's house on their imaginary superspy sledges.

"Record speed," gasped Max as they ran up the path to her house.

The door opened before Ben could knock. A woman in a dressing gown stood there. She had a box of tissues under one arm, her eyes were streaming and her nose was red and sore.

"Hello, boys," she croaked. "Dank you so mudge. My liddle darlings need a walk but I can't go out." She turned and called, "Fluffy! Bruno! Walkies . . ." then burst into a fit of coughing.

There was a soft tapping sound on the wooden floor and a tiny white dog trotted up, wagging its tail.

"Say hello to the dice boys, Fluffy."

The boys looked at each other in dismay. Fluffy was the sort of dog that girls would walk, not superspy secret agents like them.

"It looks like a feather duster," Max whispered to Ben. "We can't be seen out with that."

Fluffy sat up on her hind legs and waved her dainty paws at them.

"Bruno!" wheezed Mrs MacDonald. "Here, boy."

WOOF! A deep bark echoed around the hall and thundering steps could be heard crashing down the stairs.

Then a huge Great Dane came sliding across the floor. Fluffy jumped out of the way
just in
time as
Bruno
hurtled past
and disappeared
into the lounge.
There was an
excited whine and
then he was back, tail
wagging, buffeting the
boys with his big wet nose.

"Now that's a dog fit for superspies!" gasped Max.

Mrs MacDonald clipped the leads onto the collars of her excited dogs and handed them over to the boys.

Ben grabbed Bruno's so Max had to take Fluffy.

"They lub the park," Mrs MacDonald
told them. "Just keep them on their leads."
She bent down and patted the two dogs.
"Dow, Fluffy-wuffy and Brunikins, be
good liddle doggies!"

"I've just had an idea," said Max as Fluffy scampered along the pavement, trying to keep up with Bruno. "I bet the gargoylz would love to see the dogs. We can go past the church on our way to the park."

"Awesome!" agreed Ben.

The boys hadn't gone far up the church path when a monkey face popped up from behind a headstone.

"Greetingz!"

"Hello, Toby," said Max. "We've brought some friends to see you. And it's all right because they're not human."

Toby flew over. Fluffy jumped up, knocked him to the ground and licked his face.

"Spluttering gutterz!" chuckled Toby. "You are a friendly friend."

Pop!
Zack appeared on Bruno's back.
He reached forward and scratched behind the dog's ears. Bruno wagged his tail, wriggling his whole bottom so hard that Zack fell off into a thistle patch.

"Nice doggy," he said as he climbed out dizzily.

A stripy gargoyle with cat ears scuttled down from the church roof. He stared nervously at the dogs.

"Hello, Theo," said Ben. "Don't worry, Fluffy and Bruno won't hurt you."

"I'm not scared!" Theo made a big show of cleaning his whiskers – safely behind Max's legs. "I just don't want to scare them. They wouldn't like it if I used my special power and turned into a fierce tiger."

Max gave Ben a wink. Theo always thought he could turn into a fierce tiger, but as he was a young gargoyle, just four hundred and twelve years old, he only ever managed to become a sweet little kitten.

Bruno dragged Ben over to a stone angel, where he had a good sniff. Then he pulled him through a holly bush and off across the grass.

"I'm just letting him explore," Ben explained as he ran helplessly past his friends.

Bruno suddenly stopped at a twisted old tree, cocked his leg and did a wee against the gnarled trunk. Max and the gargoylz ran up.

"Oi!" came a creaky shout. "Mind what you're doing."

"Hide, gargoylz," hissed Max. "Sounds like the vicar's coming."

But to the boys' surprise the gargoylz just stood there grinning.

"That wasn't the vicar," said Toby.

Puzzled, Ben looked around. Toby was right. There was no one in sight.

"Then who was it?" said Ben, leaning on the old tree.

"Mind my bark!" came the voice again.

Ben jumped back. "That tree just spoke to me."

"That's not a tree," said Toby. "It's Abel. He's a gargoyle. His secret power is turning into a tree. He hasn't been in his gargoyle form for a while."

"About a hundred years," added Zack.

"Wow!" exclaimed Max, peering up at the gnarled branches. Now that he was looking hard, he could just make out the shape of a face in the knobbly trunk — two twinkly eyes, a knot for a nose and a curly slit in the bark for a grinning mouth.

"Greetingz, Abel," Toby shouted up. "We were wondering if you'd like to turn back into a gargoyle so that we can introduce you to Max and Ben properly."

There was an anxious fluttering of leaves. "But they're humanz!" said the tree in a whisper.

"It's all right," added Theo quickly. "They're our friendz. And they like playing tricks."

Max and Ben looked hopefully at the tree.

"Nothing's happening," said Max,
disappointed.

"I hope he's not cross because he got
poked and weed on . . ." Ben began.

But just then the leaves on the old
tree began to wriggle and the branches
started bending and shrinking. Then they
heard a sudden shudder and a creak, and
there in front of them stood a craggy
little gargoyle. His stone was
gnarled like bark, his
friendly face was
covered in oak
leaves and he
had twiggy
fingers
and toes.

Abel
gave a
huge
stretch.

"Dangling drainpipes, that feels nice,"
he said. "I've been a tree for so long, I'd
forgotten what it was like to move about."

He hopped from one knobbly foot to
the other.

"He's got pins and needlz," explained
Toby.

"Pins and
pine needlz,
you mean,"
said Abel with
a grin.

"I've
just had a
brilliant idea,"
said Max.
"We're taking the dogs to the park. Why
don't you come as well?"

"It's still early," said Ben, looking up
at the clock on the church tower. "So the
park should be empty . . ."

". . . and you'll be able to come without

being seen," finished Max.

"Soundz good to me," said Abel. "I'll be able to see some different treez. It's a bit boring here after a hundred yearz."

"We'll see you there," cried Zack, and with a **pop!** he disappeared.

"Meet us by the fountain," yelled Ben as the gargoylz scampered away.

The gargoylz were already waiting when the boys reached the fountain.

"Can I take Bruno's lead?" asked Toby.

"All right," said Ben, handing it over. "But hold on tight. He's very strong."

"I will," said Toby.

"This is going to be even more fun than the time when Theo **miaowed** through the vicar's sermon and he thought he had cats in his belfry!"

"My turn next! My turn next," Zack chanted, running round the fountain. Bruno took one look at the zoomy little gargoyle and leaped eagerly after him, barking madly and dragging Toby along behind.

"He's playing Chase," said Max.

"Doggy disaster!" cried Zack.

He darted for the safety of a bush,
Bruno close on his heels.

"Stop!" yelled
Toby, pulling hard
on the lead.

But Bruno
wouldn't stop. He
was going so fast
that Toby was
pulled into the air
behind him.

"He looks like
he's water-skiing!"
exclaimed Max.

"Air-skiing!" added
Ben.

"Help!" yelled Toby,
flapping his wings wildly.

"Help!" yelled Zack.

Bruno had almost caught up with the
terrified little gargoyle, his big tongue
hanging out, ready to give him a big lick.

"Come on," cried Max. He scooped Fluffy up and sprinted after Bruno and the gargoylz, Ben close on his heels. "We've got to rescue them both."

"Go invisible, Zack," shouted Ben as they chased after them through a flowerbed. "Bruno can't chase you if he can't see you."

Pop! Zack vanished, then **pop!** he reappeared.

"I'm too scared!" he yelped, weaving in and out of a row of lupins and heading for the fountain again.

"I'll stop that dog," called Theo, "with my fierce tiger pounce." He gave a loud miaow, wriggled into his kitten form and leaped at the charging Great Dane. Bruno took no notice of the little ball of stripy fur that sailed over his head and landed in the fountain with a splash.

"I think I slowed him down," said Theo, scrambling out and shaking water off his fur.

"No you didn't!" yelled Zack desperately.

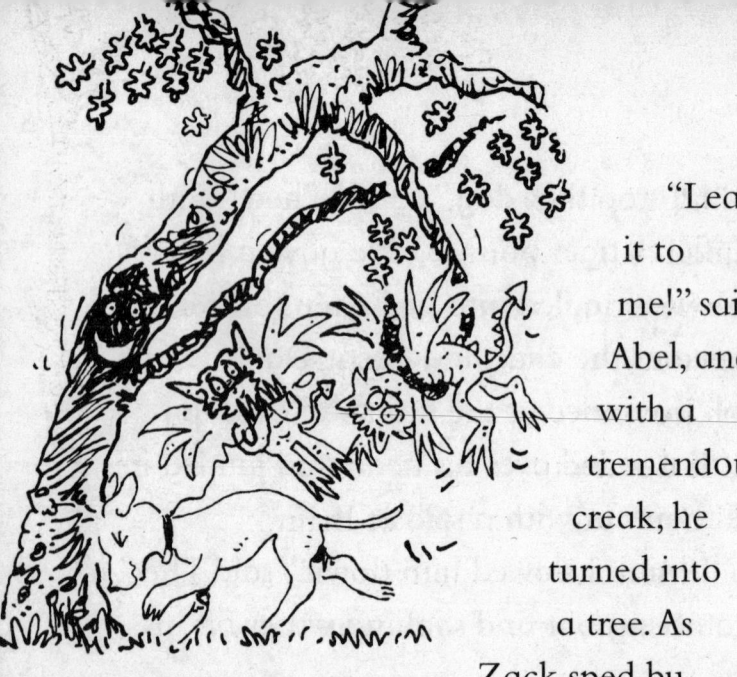

"Leaf it to me!" said Abel, and with a tremendous creak, he turned into a tree. As Zack sped by, he reached out a branch and hooked him up to safety.

Poor Bruno couldn't stop. He crashed into Abel's trunk, then sat up, looking very confused.

Toby, still holding the end of the lead, flew around and around the tree gargoyle, until Bruno was pinned to the trunk. Then he collapsed dizzily to the ground.

"Well done, Abel," said Max as he ran up. "That was quick thinking."

"Did you like my joke?" asked Abel.

"I said '*Leaf* it to me'
instead of 'Leave it to
me'. Because I'm a
tree, you see,
with leaves."

"It was very funny,"
said Ben, grabbing hold of Bruno's
lead. "Are you all right, Zack?"

Zack was sitting in the top
branches with a huge grin on his face.
"That was fun. Let's do it again!"

"No!" yelled Max and Ben together.

"We've got to give these dogs a good
walk before we take them home," said
Ben.

"My turn to take Bruno's lead,"
declared Theo.

"No way!" Ben told him. "I'm holding
it and that's that!"

"If you gargoylz were in charge, Bruno
would probably take us all to the North
Pole!" added Max.

They set off across the grass. Ben
kept Bruno ahead so he couldn't see the
gargoylz and get excited all over again.
Zack walked along beside Fluffy. They
took it in turns to jump over each other in
a sort of leapfrog.

"I've been thinking," said Toby.
Us gargoylz should get a dog."

"You couldn't keep it on the church
roof though," said Max doubtfully.

"I've got a better idea," declared Ben.
"We'll ask if we can walk Bruno and
Fluffy another day."

"Awesome!" said Max.

"*Paw*some, you mean!" chuckled Abel.

4. Gargoyle Racers

Max leaped eagerly out of bed, slid down the banister and burst into the kitchen.

"What exciting plans have you got for me today?" he asked his mum as he tucked into a huge bowl of Chocowheats.

His mother was sorting through some papers. She looked harassed. "I've been far too busy to organize anything," she said. "Jessica's tidying her bedroom. You could help her."

Max groaned. He couldn't think of anything worse.

"Or you can hang out the washing," suggested Mrs Black.

Max grabbed his toast and scarpered. Maybe tidying his sister's bedroom wouldn't be so bad after all. He'd just thought of a secret plan . . .

"Mum!" shrieked Jessica ten minutes later. "Max has ruined my bedroom!"

Mrs Black came charging up the stairs. Max was standing in the middle of Jessica's room, looking very pleased with himself.

All Jessica's dolls were now standing on their heads, hanging from the curtains or stuffed upside down in her fluffy pink slippers. One was swinging from the lampshade.

"I was making her room look more exciting," explained Max. "You can't please some people!"

His mother sighed. "Follow me," she said wearily.

"I'm not doing any more dusting or washing up," Max told her as he mooched down the stairs after her. "Too much housework is bad for kids."

Mrs Black strode into the lounge, dived into her enormous handbag and pulled out some crumpled bits of paper. "I got these free with some washing powder," she said, handing them to Max.

Puzzled, Max straightened them out. "Two go-karting vouchers!" he yelled in delight. "Thanks, Mum. Just right for Ben and me. I'll phone him now."

Half an hour later Max and Ben were
waving goodbye to Ben's mum at the
entrance to Kart World. They handed over
their vouchers and dashed through the
gate. Shiny go-karts were lined up in a
lay-by next to the circuit.

"I'm having that kart!" came a
menacing voice.

Max's radar sprang to life: shaved head, big fists, safety helmet with KING OF THE KARTERS written on it. He knew what that meant. It was Enemy Agent Barry Price, also known as The Basher, codename: School Bully.

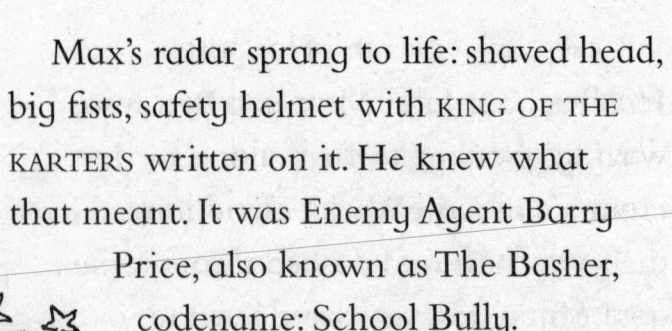

Barry pushed three children out of the way and climbed into a shiny black kart with red flames painted along the sides.

"I always take number twelve," he was telling everyone loudly. "Fastest kart in the place. No one

can keep up with me." He spotted Max
and Ben. "Especially not you two losers."
With that he zoomed off along the track,
leaving a cloud of dust behind him.

"I forgot that The Basher comes go-
karting," said Ben gloomily as the boys
walked along the racks of safety helmets.
"I hope he's not going to spoil everything."

"We'll keep away from him," said Max.
He took down a helmet to try it on and a
squat, stony shape popped up behind it.

"Greetingz!" came a growly purr.
"Toby!" exclaimed Max in delight.

"How did you know we were here?"

"I followed Ben's mum's car when it went past the church," Toby told him.

"So did we," said Azzan and Eli, crawling out from under a pile of rubber tyres.

"We had to run really quickly," Eli said in his hissy voice. The wriggling snakes on his head pretended to pant.

"It wasss a good thing there wasss that traffic jam otherwise we'd never have kept up."

"Abel's here too," Toby added, pointing out a gnarled old tree on the side of the track.

"Which one isss *my* kart?" asked Eli, rubbing his paws together eagerly while his snakes hissed in excitement.

"You can't have your own go-karts . . ." said Ben.

The gargoylz' faces fell.

". . . but you can all ride with us!" Max added quickly.

Toby, Azzan and Eli gave a great cheer and scuttled off to the karts. Soon Toby was hidden inside Ben's car – number six – and Eli and Azzan were squeezed in at Max's feet in number nine.

Vroom! No sooner had they set off down the track than Barry shot past.

"Can't you go faster than that, sluggy slowcoaches?" he shouted.

"We'll show him, Agent Neal," said Max, slamming his foot hard down on the accelerator.

"This is fantastic, Agent Black!" yelled Ben as they sped along. "We must be travelling at supersonic spy speed. The Basher can't be going faster than this."

VROOOM! Barry's kart raced up behind them. "You're driving so slowly I thought you'd stopped," he taunted. "I'll help you go quicker."

Before the boys could do anything about it, he rammed into both their karts, sending them skidding across the track.

"What's going on?" came Toby's wobbly voice.

"We're being attacked!" cried Azzan, clinging to Max's foot. Eli's snakes started wriggling nervously.

"Keep still!" Max shouted at the gargoylz. "I'm trying to steady the kart. The Basher's giving it a bashing."

"Look at Max," Barry called to the other drivers. "He's so scared he's talking to his toes!"

As Max opened his mouth to protest, a voice came over the loudspeaker:

"Cars six, nine and twelve – this is not a bumper-car track. Take five minutes in the pits for messing about."

"We might have known Barry would get us into trouble," Max muttered to Ben.

They drove into the lay-by where they'd started and plonked themselves on the bench that looked out over the circuit.

Barry stomped over and sat down next to them, almost pushing them off the end. "I'm losing go-karting time, thanks to you two," he moaned.

"We didn't do anything!" protested Max. "You were the one who bumped into us."

"You blocked me," he insisted.

They all sat there gloomily, waiting for their five minutes' punishment to be up.

"At least this didn't get squished," whispered Ben, pulling a small green ball out of his pocket. "It's a super-powerful stink bomb. I'm going to use it on Arabella later."

"Great idea," said Max.

"She always gets on the PlayStation first after tea," Ben explained, "playing some stupid girly game. I'm going to stink her out – then I can have a go on Evil Robot Attack – nose peg firmly in place, of course."

He was just about to put the stink bomb away when The Basher snatched it out of his hand.

"Give that back, Barry!" protested Ben.

But at that moment the loudspeaker burst into life. "Karts six, nine and twelve – time out finished."

Barry jumped up and ran off towards his go-kart. He waved the stink bomb in the air. "I've decided to let you have it back . . ." he told Ben.

"Thanks, Barry!" said Ben.

". . . if you can beat me on that obstacle course there," Barry added, pointing to a separate

loop of track, "and you'll never do that.
No one can beat the King of the Karters!"

Ben looked over at the obstacle course.
It was a circular track with two lines of
cones, a figure of eight and a long dark
tunnel. "The Basher's probably done this a
hundred times," he muttered. "I'll never get
my stink bomb back."

"Yes you will, Agent Neal," Max told
him in a low voice. "With a little help
from the gargoylz, of course." He winked

at Ben. "Secret Plan: Win the Obstacle Race."

"I like your thinking, Agent Black," said Ben, cheering up at once.

Max whistled to the gargoylz. Toby, Azzan and Eli came scampering over and ducked down behind the bench near Max and Ben. Max told them about the race.

Azzan breathed an excited burst of fire. "We'll certainly help!" he agreed. "I'll wait in the tunnel." He ran off and disappeared into the dark.

"I'll stay by the cones," said Toby.

"And I'll tell Abel what we're up to!" said Eli. "He'll want to help." In a second he'd used his special power, turned into a long wriggling snake and slithered away.

"It's a risky mission, Agent Neal," said Max, giving Ben a solemn pat on the back. "Good luck."

"I'm going to need it if I want my stink bomb back, Agent Black," whispered Ben. "I'm depending on the gargoylz."

"Hurry up!" called Barry. He was in his go-kart now, revving his engine. "We'll start the race here."

Ben ran over and jumped into his kart.

Max pulled out his mobile phone. "I'll be judge," he called to Barry. "I'll take a photo at the end so that we can see who wins."

"No need," sneered Barry. "I'll be so far ahead that Ben won't even be in the same picture."

"Ready, steady . . ." began Max.

Before he had a chance to shout go, The Basher zoomed off, heading towards

the obstacle course at top speed. He wove
expertly in and out of his line of cones.

Ben set off as fast as he could while
Max ran over to the side of the track. Ben
had reached the cones now. Max slapped
a hand over his eyes. He couldn't bear to
watch. Ben was going so fast there was no
way he could steer round the cones.

But then he heard a shout of triumph from his friend. He peered through his fingers – and burst out laughing. Toby was moving the cones out of the way so that Ben didn't hit any of them. Ben shot straight ahead. He was catching up with Barry now!

The figure of eight was next. It wound its way among a clump of tall trees. Ben saw that Abel had taken root on the edge of them, his branches overhanging the track.

With a screech of tyres, The Basher pulled ahead. He was about to take the bend right by Abel when something suddenly swung down in front of his face.

It was green and yellow and hissed menacingly at him.

"It's Eli!" gasped Max.

Barry let out a yell of terror and yanked the steering wheel to avoid the

grinning snake. The kart whizzed through the thick bushes on the side of the track, sending up a shower of leaves.

Ben took his chance. He zoomed past
Barry, who was now emerging from the
bushes with twigs in his hair.

"That's not fair," yelled The Basher,
trying to catch up again. "There was a
snake! It nearly swallowed me whole."

"I didn't see one!" Ben shouted over his
shoulder. *At least, not a real* one, he added

to himself. *Gargoyle snakes don't count.*

There was only the tunnel to go now. Ben suddenly realized he could win the race — and then he'd get his stink bomb back!

But just then he felt a sharp jolt as Barry's kart tried to knock him off the track.

His heart sank. The Basher had caught up! He'd forgotten that number twelve was the fastest kart.

Ben gripped the steering wheel tightly

and aimed for the mouth of the tunnel.

With his foot down hard on the accelerator, he fixed his eyes on the semicircle of light at the other end. Beyond it he could see Max standing at the finishing line, cheering him on.

But he could hear The Basher roaring up behind.

"Barry Price, champion karter, does it again!" Barry was yelling. "Prepare to be overtaken, loser."

Then something dropped onto the back of Ben's kart. It was Azzan!

"Gargoyle to the rescue!" he declared, taking in a huge breath.

Barry was whooping with delight as he prepared to overtake. His kart was sitting right on Ben's tail now. "It's going to be a great win," he cried. "A spectacular last-minute— *Bleugh!*" Barry started coughing as Azzan breathed out a huge cloud of black smoke, right in his face. Choking and wheezing, he zigzagged along the tunnel, bumping blindly into the walls as Ben shot ahead.

"The winner!" yelled
Max, taking a photo as
Ben drove over the finishing
line, arms in the air, and came
to a halt.

Eli and Abel – who had turned
back into gargoylz to watch the
finish – bounded onto the kart. Toby
flew down to join them and they all
did a victory dance on the bonnet.

There was an angry shout from the
tunnel. A sooty Basher was driving slowly
out of the smoke.

"He doesn't look too happy," chortled
Eli.

SNAP! Max took a photo.

"He looks a bit snappy to me," said
Abel.

"Good pun!" cried Toby.

Chuckling, the gargoylz hid inside
Ben's kart. Max and Ben tried to keep
their faces straight as Barry Price made
his way to the finishing line. He climbed
out of his grimy vehicle and stomped
towards the boys.

"I won the race," said Ben. "You have
to give me my stink bomb back now."

"No way!" snapped The Basher. He
waved the green ball in the boys' faces.

"I'm keeping it. I'll use it to stink out someone who deserves it. You'd better hope it's not you two."

Max and Ben weren't taking any chances in the face of the super-powerful stink bomb. They backed away quickly. Then they heard the loudspeaker crackle into life.

"Numbers six and nine, please return your karts. Your session is over."

"Oh no," gasped Max. "It can't be."

Barry gave a nasty laugh. "I don't have to stop. My mum's paid for the whole day."

With that, he thrust the stink bomb into his back pocket and leaped into his kart. Immediately a dreadful smell wafted out. He'd sat on the stink bomb!

Laughing helplessly, Max and Ben

drove off
towards the
kiosk, leaving
Barry gasping
and flapping his
arms as if he were
trying to take off.

"The Basher certainly
stank out someone who deserved
it," chuckled Max. "Himself!"

Toby's head popped up from Ben's kart.
"Dangling drainpipes!" he exclaimed. "I
haven't laughed so much since Barney did
a bottom burp in the vicar's fridge and he
thought his cheese had gone off."

"Shame I won't get to play on the
PlayStation," said Ben. "But it was worth
it to see Barry turn into a stink bum."

Abel clapped his twiggy hands together.
"Very clever joke, Ben." He turned to the
other gargoylz. "Do you see what he did?
He said stink *bum* instead of stink *bomb*.

I love a good pun."

"And I've got a brilliant idea that will solve your PlayStation problem," Max told Ben. "We'll just get Barney to do a smell under Arabella's chair instead."

"And when she's been stunk out, we can all play Evil Robot Attack," declared Ben.

"Yippee!" yelled the gargoylz.

"I'll bring some extra nose pegs," said Max.

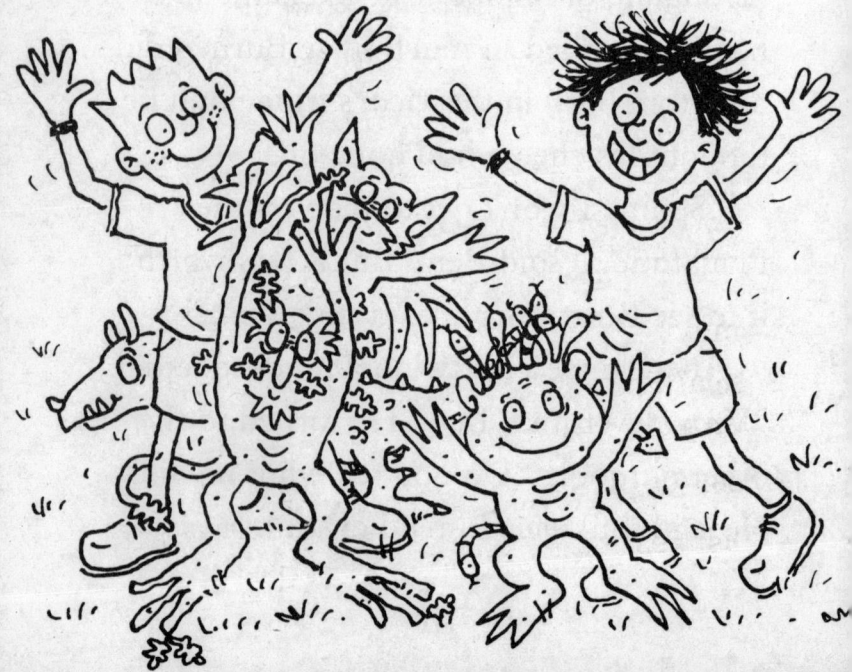

Gargoylz Fact File

Full name: Tobias the Third
Known as: Toby
Special Power: Flying
Likes: All kinds of pranks and mischief – especially playing jokes on the vicar
Dislikes: Mrs Hogsbottom, garden gnomes

Full name: Barnabas
Known as: Barney
Special Power: Making big stinks!
Likes: Cookiez
Dislikes: Being surprised by humanz

Name: Eli
Special Power: Turning into a grass snake
Likes: Sssports Day, Ssslithering
Dislikes: Ssscary ssstories

Full name: Bartholomew

Known as: Bart

Special Power: Burping spiders

Likes: Being grumpy

Dislikes: Being told to cheer up

Full name: Theophilus

Known as: Theo

Special Power: Turning into a ferocious tiger (well, tabby kitten!)

Likes: Sunny spots and cosy places

Dislikes: Rain

Full name: Zackary

Known as: Zack

Special Power: Making himself invisible to humanz

Likes: Bouncing around, eating bramblz, thistlz, and anything with pricklz!

Dislikes: Keeping still

Full name: Nebuchadnezzar
Known as: Neb
Special Power: Changing colour to match his background
Likes: Snorkelling
Dislikes: Anyone treading on his tail

Name: Azzan
Special Power: Breathing fire
Likes: Surprises
Dislikes: Smoke going up his nose and making him sneeze

Full name: Abel
Special Power: Turning into a tree
Likes: Funny puns and word jokes
Dislikes: Dogs weeing up against him

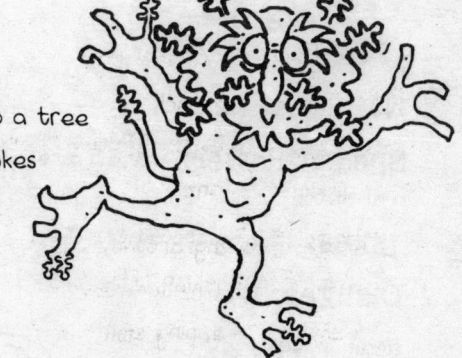

Full name: Jehieli
Known as: Jelly
Special Power: Turning to jelly
Likes: Having friendz to play with
Dislikes: Bulliez and spoilsports

Name: Ira
Special Power: Making it rain
Likes: Making humanz walk the plank
Dislikes: Being bored

Name: Cyrus
Special Power: Singing lullabies to send humanz to sleep
Likes: Fun dayz out
Dislikes: Snoring

Name: Rufus
Special Power: Turning into a skeleton
Likes: Playing spooky tricks
Dislikes: Squeezing into small spaces

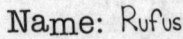